W9-APE-685

If you're not from the prairie...

For my Mom and Dad, who, unlike so many others, chose to remain on the prairies.

—David Bouchard

To the memory of my parents, Christian and Philomena Ripplinger, prairie pioneers.

—Henry Ripplinger

If you're not from the prairie…

DAVID BOUCHARD
Story

HENRY RIPPLINGER
Images

If you're not from the prairie…

Aladdin Paperbacks

If you're not from the prairie,
You don't know the sun,
You *can't* know the sun.

Diamonds that bounce off crisp winter snow,
Warm waters in dugouts and lakes that we know.
The sun is our friend from when we are young,
A child of the prairie is part of the sun.

If you're not from the prairie,
You *don't* know the sun.

If you're not from the prairie,
You don't know the wind,
You can't know the wind.

Our cold winds of winter cut right to the core,
Hot summer wind devils can blow down the door.
As children we know when we play any game,
The wind will be there, yet we play just the same.

If you're not from the prairie,
You don't know the wind.

If you're not from the prairie,
You don't know the sky,
You *can't* know the sky.

The bold prairie sky is clear, bright and blue,
Though sometimes cloud messages give us a clue.
Monstrous grey mushrooms can hint of a storm,
Or painted pink feathers say goodbye to the warm.

If you're not from the prairie,
You *don't* know the sky.

If you're not from the prairie,
You don't know what's flat,
You've *never* seen flat.

When travellers pass through across our great plain,
They all view our home, they all say the same:
"It's simple and flat!" They've not learned to see,
The particular beauty that's now part of me.

If you're not from the prairie,
You *don't* know what's flat.

If you're not from the prairie,
You've not heard the grass,
You've never *heard* grass.

In strong summer winds, the grains and grass bend
And sway to a dance that seems never to end.
It whispers its secrets — they tell of this land
And the rhythm of life played by nature's own hand.

If you're not from the prairie,
You've never *heard* grass.

So you're not from the prairie,
And yet you know snow.
You *think* you know snow?

Blizzards bring danger, as legends have told,
In deep drifts we roughhouse, ignoring the cold.
At times we look out at great seas of white,
So bright is the sun that we squeeze our eyes tight.

If you're not from the prairie,
You *don't* know snow.

If you're not from the prairie,
You don't know our trees,
You *can't* know our trees.

The trees that we know have taken so long,
To live through our seasons, to grow tall and strong.
They're loved and they're treasured, we watched as they grew,
We knew they were special — the prairie has few.

If you're not from the prairie,
You *don't* know our trees.

Still, you're not from the prairie,
And yet you know cold....
You say you've *been* cold?

Of all of those memories we share when we're old,
None are more clear than that hard bitter cold.
You'll not find among us a soul who can say:
"I've conquered the wind on a cold winter's day."

If you're not from the prairie,
You *don't* know the cold,
You've *never* been cold!

If you're not from the prairie,

You don't know me.

You just can't know *ME*.

You see,

My hair's mostly wind,

My eyes filled with grit,

My skin's red or brown,

My lips chapped and split.

I've lain on the prairie and heard grasses sigh.

I've stared at the vast open bowl of the sky.

I've seen all those castles and faces in clouds,

My home is the prairie, and I cry out loud.

If you're not from the prairie, you can't know my soul,

You don't know our blizzards, you've not fought our cold.

You can't know my mind, nor ever my heart,

Unless deep within you, there's somehow a part....

A part of these things that I've said that I know,

The wind, sky and earth, the storms and the snow.

Best say you have — and then we'll be one,

For we will have shared that same blazing sun.

First Aladdin Paperbacks edition June 1998

Text copyright © 1995 by David Bouchard
Illustrations copyright © 1995 by Henry Ripplinger

Aladdin Paperbacks
An imprint of Simon & Schuster
Children's Publishing Division
1230 Avenue of the Americas
New York, NY 10020

Originally published in Canada by Raincoast Book Distribution Ltd.
First United States edition 1995

All rights reserved including the right of
reproduction in whole or in part in any form.

Also available in an Atheneum Books for Young Readers hardcover edition.

Book design by Ken Budd

The text of this book is set in Adobe Garamond.
The illustrations were done in acrylic.

Manufactured in China

13 15 17 19 20 18 16 14

Library of Congress Catalog Card Number: 94-78306
ISBN 0-689-80103-3 (Atheneum)
ISBN 0-689-82035-6 (Aladdin pbk.)